AMAZON®:

How Jeff Bezos Built the World's Largest Online Store

WIZARDS OF TECHNOLOGY

Amazon®: How Jeff Bezos Built the World's Largest Online Store

Disney's Pixar®: How Steve Jobs Changed Hollywood

Facebook®: How Mark Zuckerberg Connected More Than a Billion Friends

Google®: How Larry Page & Sergey Brin Changed the Way We Search the Web

Instagram®: How Kevin Systrom & Mike Krieger Changed the Way We Take and Share Photos

Netflix®: How Reed Hastings Changed the Way We Watch Movies & TV

Pinterest®: How Ben Silbermann & Evan Sharp Changed the Way We Share What We Love

Tumblr®: How David Karp Changed the Way We Blog

Twitter®: How Jack Dorsey Changed the Way We Communicate

YouTube®: How Steve Chen Changed the Way We Watch Videos

WIZARDS OF TECHNOLOGY

AMAZON®:
How Jeff Bezos Built the World's Largest Online Store

AURELIA JACKSON

Mason Crest
450 Parkway Drive, Suite D
Broomall, PA 19008
www.masoncrest.com

Copyright © 2015 by Mason Crest, an imprint of National Highlights, Inc. All rights reserved. No part of this publication may be reproduced or transmitted in any form or by any means, electronic or mechanical, including photocopying, recording, taping, or any information storage and retrieval system, without permission from the publisher.

Printed and bound in the United States of America.

First printing
9 8 7 6 5 4 3 2 1

Series ISBN: 978-1-4222-3178-4
ISBN: 978-1-4222-3179-1
ebook ISBN: 978-1-4222-8715-6

Library of Congress Cataloging-in-Publication Data

Jackson, Aurelia.
 Amazon(tm) : how Jeff Bezos built the world's largest online store / Aurelia Jackson.
    pages cm. — (Wizards of technology)
 ISBN 978-1-4222-3179-1 (hardback) — ISBN 978-1-4222-3178-4 (series) — ISBN 978-1-4222-8715-6 (ebook) 1. Bezos, Jeffrey—Juvenile literature. 2. Amazon.com (Firm)—History—Juvenile literature. 3. Booksellers and bookselling--United States—Biography—Juvenile literature. 4. Businessmen—United States--Biography—Juvenile literature. 5. Internet bookstores—United States—History—Juvenile literature. 6. Electronic commerce—United States—History—Juvenile literature. I. Title. II. Title: Amazon trademark. III. Title: Amazon.
 Z473.B47J33 2014
 381'.4500202854678—dc23
 [B]
                                    2014012226

CONTENTS

1. New Ideas   7
2. Dominating Book Sales   21
3. Expansion   33
4. Moving Forward   47
Find Out More   59
Series Glossary of Key Terms   60
Index   62
About the Author and Picture Credits   64

KEY ICONS TO LOOK FOR:

Text-Dependent Questions: These questions send the reader back to the text for more careful attention to the evidence presented there.

Words to Understand: These words with their easy-to-understand definitions will increase the reader's understanding of the text, while building vocabulary skills.

Series Glossary of Key Terms: This back-of-the book glossary contains terminology used throughout this series. Words found here increase the reader's ability to read and comprehend higher-level books and articles in this field.

Research Projects: Readers are pointed toward areas of further inquiry connected to each chapter. Suggestions are provided for projects that encourage deeper research and analysis.

Sidebars: This boxed material within the main text allows readers to build knowledge, gain insights, explore possibilities, and broaden their perspectives by weaving together additional information to provide realistic and holistic perspectives.

Words to Understand

warehouse: A large building where products are stored, ready to be shipped somewhere else.
technological: Having to do with things that people invent.
electronic: Using electricity or battery power to work.
distribution: Getting the things you sell to the people who want to buy them.

CHAPTER ONE

New Ideas

As strange as it may seem today, the Internet didn't become a part of most people's lives until the 1990s. About that time, companies began selling products online, and online businesses also quickly became a part of our lives. Most companies still had normal stores built out of bricks and cement in addition to their online stores, though—stores that stood on city streets where people could come in and shop.

In 1994, Jeff Bezos started a different kind of business: Amazon.com, a digital bookstore. Unlike other businesses, Amazon had no physical store where people could go inside a building and look at the books lined up on shelves. Instead, every book Amazon sold had to be bought online.

What began as a simple online bookstore eventually blossomed into

8 AMAZON

Jeff Bezos' big ideas have changed the way people shop for the things they need. Today, Amazon is one of the most successful businesses on the Internet, but the company had humble beginnings.

New Ideas 9

one of the largest online stores in existence. Customers from all over the world could now buy all sorts of products from Amazon.com, ranging from books to clothes and food and even health care products. However, the company never forgot its roots. Books have always been one of Amazon's top priorities.

Before Amazon, most books were purchased in bookstores—but Jeff's website allowed customers to order books online, which opened a whole new world of possibility for people from all around the world. People no longer had to depend on their local bookstores to get them the books they wanted. They didn't have to use mail-order catalogs for hard-to-find books either. Where once book buyers would have had to wait for a week or more for books to be shipped to them, now customers could receive a book ordered through Amazon.com much more quickly.

There are many reasons Amazon is successful, but one of the most important is its ability to adapt to a changing world. The future of products will continue to change with the digital age. Companies like Amazon will need to continue to adapt in order to be successful.

STARTING OUT

One of the best words to describe Jeff Bezos is innovative. Innovative people see a changing world and develop new ideas or methods to fit

Make Connections

When you see ".com" at the end of a website, it's short for "commerce." It means that the website belongs to a business. Other website endings include ".edu," for schools and colleges; ".gov," for government organizations; and ".net" for other sorts of online organizations.

10 AMAZON

When Jeff started Amazon, few people used the Internet to shop. Amazon helped to change the way people thought about shopping online.

New Ideas   11

that changing world. In the early 1990s, the world's use of computers was growing fast. Personal computers, which had once been very expensive, were now becoming more affordable for everyday people. By the middle of the 1990s, almost everyone had a home computer.

Jeff Bezos saw a great opportunity, and he knew it was only a matter of time before other people saw it too. If he were going to take advantage of this idea, he would have to act fast.

Jeff's willingness to try new things started when he was still young. He was born on January 12, 1964, in Albuquerque, New Mexico, to a teenage mother, Jacklyn Gise Jorgensen, and his biological father, Ted Jorgensen. His parents were married less than a year, though, and when Jeff was four years old, his mother married Mike Bezos, a Cuban immigrant.

As a child, Jeff wanted to understand how things work. He turned his parents' garage into a laboratory, and he built electrical contraptions around his house. Later, as a teenager, he developed a love for computers. His family moved to Miami, Florida, where Jeff did well in school. In high school, he started his first business, the Dream Institute, an educational summer camp for fourth, fifth and sixth graders. He graduated as the valedictorian of his class.

When Jeff went to college at Princeton University, he decided to pursue his interest in computers there. He graduated with honors in 1986 with a degree in computer science and electrical engineering. After graduation, he found work in the business world on Wall Street. Eventually, he ended up at the investment firm D. E. Shaw, where he met his wife Mackenzie. He was named the youngest vice president at D. E. Shaw in 1990.

Jeff took a huge risk when he decided to leave his job the investment firm, but he knew he needed to devote himself full-time to his new project if it was going to be successful. His college background meant he was already very skilled at managing websites, and building a website that would allow users to buy products would not be hard for him. Learning how to run a business, however, was something completely new to him.

12 AMAZON

While bookstores have a limited amount of shelf space for books, Amazon can offer an almost endless number of titles for customers to search through.

New Ideas   13

AMAZON IS BORN

There are a lot of decisions to be made while starting up a new business. One of the first challenges Jeff faced was choosing what to sell. He hoped to sell all sorts of products one day, but he also knew he would have to choose one product to start out with. Selling everything at once would be far too difficult. Jeff came up with a list of five products he thought would sell well online: compact discs (or CDs), computer hardware, computer software, videos, and books.

Books seemed like the perfect place for Jeff to start. Even the largest bookstores at the time could only hold a certain amount of books. Customers looking for a less common book would need to ask the bookstore to order the book for them. Buying books online offered a faster, and sometimes cheaper, alternative. Best of all, customers wouldn't have to wait for a store to be open to do it. They could log on to a website at all hours of the day and night and buy a book instantly. Jeff envisioned his website selling every book a customer would ever want.

The second choice Jeff needed to make was where he would start his business. He had lived in New York before he quit his job, but Jeff needed to find a location near a *warehouse* that sold and shipped all kinds of books to retail bookstores. That way, he would be able to send the books straight to the customers in record time.

The West Coast of the United States seemed like a great place to settle down. Plenty of other *technological* businesses were opening up there, which had led to a part of California becoming known as Silicon Valley. (Silicon is a type of metal used in *electronic* chips.) At first, Jeff considered Silicon Valley a great place to start a business that relied on the Internet, but he decided against it because of how tax laws worked.

Costumers living in the state where an online business was located would need to pay sales tax. This meant that Californians would be forced to pay more money, while customers living in other states would

14 AMAZON

One of the early hurdles in Amazon's rise to success was finding enough warehouse space to keep up with customer demand.

New Ideas   15

Jeff decided to start Amazon in Seattle to base the company near an Oregon book distribution center. Jeff had an easier time finding tech-smart employees in Seattle as well.

not have to. The state of California has a very large population. Jeff feared he would lose a lot of his California customers to other businesses if he stationed his warehouse in Silicon Valley.

    Jeff began his search for another location. He finally settled on Seattle, Washington, a city is located in the northwestern corner of the United States. Jeff hoped it would be the perfect location for his new business for two reasons: it was close to a large book **distribution** center in Oregon, and plenty of people trained in technology lived in the area. That way, Jeff would have no trouble finding employees to work for him.

16 AMAZON

Before Jeff could take over online shopping with Amazon.com, he had to start with a business plan. Every successful company starts with a business plan.

New Ideas   17

Text-Dependent Questions

1. According to the author, what are the five products Jeff considered selling before choosing to sell books?
2. What are the two reasons Jeff chose Seattle, Washington as the location of his new business?
3. Why did Jeff decide to name his company Cadabra? What caused him to change the name?
4. The author lists three reasons for why Jeff chose the name "Amazon" for his new company. What are they?

Starting a brand new business means taking a lot of risks. For Jeff, this meant packing his bags, saying goodbye to his life in New York City, and moving to Seattle to get his company started. The drive took days, and Jeff spent most of his time on the road working on a business plan for his new website. He had already chosen a location and a market, but now he needed to think of a name.

Jeff thought of plenty of names before he finally chose the name "Cadabra," which is a shortened form of the word "abracadabra," the word sometimes used by magicians when they're about to finish a trick. Jeff thought his website's customers would be amazed by the new service, just like a magician's talents amaze an audience. He settled on Cadabra as a good name for his new business, and Cadabra, Inc. was founded in July of 1994.

A lot of legal work goes into starting a business and building a website. Jeff started his company out of his home, but he kept in touch with a lawyer over the phone to get the legal aspects of his new business settled. One of the first topics Jeff and the lawyer spoke about over the phone was the name of the company.

When Jeff said he wanted to name his website, "Cadabra," the lawyer misheard him. He thought Jeff had said "Cadaver" instead. A cadaver

18 AMAZON

Amazon wasn't Jeff's first choice for his company's name, but it ended up being the best choice for the new online store.

New Ideas 19

Research Project

This chapter tells the story of how Amazon.com came to have the name it has. Use the Internet to research how "Kindle" got its name. Explain why this name was chosen for Amazon's e-book reader.

is a medical term for a human corpse. Jeff did not like the idea that his new company's name could be mistaken for a dead body! He decided to come up with a new name right away.

Jeff thought long and hard about a second name. After all, he didn't want to make the same mistake twice! He settled on the name Amazon because he hoped the word would symbolize his company in a number of ways. The Amazon River is the largest river in the world, and Jeff hoped his own company would become the largest online retailer. Water also flows down a river, and products from Jeff's website would "flow" to customers. The Amazon River is located in South America, which Jeff believed made the name Amazon sound exotic and foreign to people from the United States. He hoped his customers would see his website as something both exciting and new, just like the famous large river. A final reason Jeff liked the name Amazon so much is because the letter "A" is at the start of the alphabet, which meant his website would be listed toward the top of an alphabetical list when people searched for it on the Internet.

Jeff was well on his way to his new life as the owner of the greatest Internet company in the world. But there was still a lot of work to be done.

Words to Understand

stockholders: People who buy pieces of a company. Then the company can use their money to do business.

profit: Money that you make from a business, after you've paid for everything.

retailer: A business that sells things directly to the customers who will use them, instead of selling things to another company to sell again.

inventory: The products you have in storage, ready to be sold.

competition: The other companies that do the same thing your company does.

market: The people that a company sells to.

CHAPTER TWO

Dominating Book Sales

Jeff had big ideas. But now he needed to make those ideas a reality. He had to think about lots of practical things that go along with starting a business—things like money, buildings, and employees.

MONEY PLANS

Jeff was a very wealthy man. He had earned a salary of over a million dollars a year working on Wall Street in New York City. Despite his wealth, however, he didn't have the money to start a business as large as Amazon on his own. He needed to raise enough money to get the website off the ground, and that required help from others. He would need **stockholders** to invest in his company. He also needed a business plan.

AMAZON

One of the keys to Amazon's success has been the company's easy-to-use website. Before Amazon could become a successful business, customers had to enjoy using the online store.

A business plan is a little like a map for the future. It spells out the business's goals for the future and the steps it will take to reach those goals. Jeff's plan was different from most businesses, because he did not plan on his business making a **profit** for four to five years. Amazon's stockholders weren't very happy about Jeff's slow-growth plan. They wanted their investment in the company to make money more quickly. But Jeff was sure that his plan was a smart one. And it turned out he was right!

GARAGE BEGINNING

Next, Jeff needed to find a place to house his business. Amazon did not need a storefront or a large office. All Jeff really needed was a small space to get work done and ship orders. He bought a small house with

Dominating Book Sales   23

a large garage in Seattle, and he and his wife moved in. Jeff's plan was to add a few desks and computer stations to the garage and turn it into a very small office.

Amazon was not the first company to start in a garage. In fact, plenty of other very successful startup companies had done the exact same thing. Jeff wanted to follow in their footsteps so that he could say Amazon came from humble beginnings, too. One of the most famous examples of companies that began in a garage is Apple Computers.

Of course, Jeff's garage was not large enough to hold all of the books he would sell online. Any orders placed on Amazon.com would be sent directly to a larger book **retailer**. That retailer would send the books in the order to Jeff's garage, where they would be packaged and shipped to the customer in just a few short days.

EMPLOYEES

Another challenge Jeff ran into while starting his company was actually building the website. Jeff knew he wouldn't be able to build it alone, so he hired two expert computer programmers named Shel Kaphan and Paul Barton-Davis. Unfortunately, neither Jeff nor his new employees knew how to run a business that sold books. They had a lot to learn! Jeff attended a class about it from the American Booksellers Association before the website was finished.

The employees of Amazon.com worked hard to ensure that the website was easy to use. It had a search function, where customers could type in a title or author of a book. All possible titles would then pop up on customers' screens, where they could select a specific book to order. Each book had its own page showing information about that book.

If selecting books to buy was easy, then paying for those books was even easier. All customers had to do to order books was enter their addresses and credit card information. Once the books were paid for, they would be shipped from the Amazon headquarters as soon as possible.

Amazon.com was officially launched in July of 1995. It was instantly

24 AMAZON

Jeff began Amazon in his garage because the company didn't need much space to operate. It wouldn't be long before Amazon would need to move into a bigger office.

Dominating Book Sales

a big hit, and received a lot of attention online. Yahoo, one of the most popular search engines at the time, listed Amazon on its "What's Cool List." Another search engine named Netscape listed Amazon on its "What's New List." This sort of exposure helped Amazon. In the first two months of business, Amazon sold to all fifty states of America and over forty-five countries around the world. Within two months, Amazon's sales were $20,000 per week!

OUTGROWING THE GARAGE

The popularity of Jeff's website was growing even faster than he could have dreamed. Jeff was finding it hard to keep up with all the newfound business.

The first version of Amazon allowed users to choose from over a million different titles, but only about two thousand books could be held in Jeff's garage at any one time. Orders needed to be shipped from Jeff's garage almost immediately after they were received for there to be enough space for all the other orders that would pass through. It wasn't long before Jeff needed to find a bigger space to store all the orders waiting to be shipped.

More space for *inventory* wasn't the only reason Jeff rented a large office in Seattle. He also needed more space for employees and the computers he needed to maintain his business. More computers were needed to handle orders, and more employees were necessary to speak with customers if they needed help. Jeff also hired employees to expand the website and the business as a whole.

Amazon.com was the first business that functioned only online, but Jeff knew he would soon have plenty of *competition*. He needed to find ways to get people to keep using his website instead of his competitors. He wanted his customers to be loyal to Amazon, so that they would shop there over and over.

One way Jeff made Amazon more popular was by offering a lot of discounts. Customers could buy books for anywhere between 10 to 30

26 AMAZON

As online shopping became more popular, Amazon became more successful. Offering the choices customers wanted and a simple website made Amazon one of the most successful early online stores.

Dominating Book Sales

Make Connections

One of the features added to Amazon was the ability to comment on a book listed on the website. This comment, known as a review, would be seen by anyone else who viewed the title. It would help other customers decide whether to buy the book or not. Being able to review a book before buying it is just one of the ways Amazon was different from a traditional bookstore. Soon other websites used the same idea.

percent more cheaply than what they would normally pay in a store. To top it all off, people who were not located in Washington didn't have to pay tax. Amazon became the cheapest and fastest way to buy books online, especially books that were not common.

The very first version of Amazon only allowed users to look up titles using the title or author. Later versions added more features, such as categories that customers could browse. Someone interested in mystery books might check out the mystery category, for example. Amazon also added a suggestion section for people who didn't know what they were looking for. These suggestions were based on titles the customer had previously viewed or bought. Amazon was becoming easier and easier for people to use.

ASSOCIATES PROGRAM

Amazon.com found yet another way to be more attractive to users in July 1996 when the company opened its "Associates Program." Now anyone who owned a website could participate. After signing up, website owners would pick a book from Amazon's website and place an advertisement for that book on their website. If someone followed that link and

28 AMAZON

Once a very small company, Amazon has expanded around the world with online stores for the United Kingdom, France, Germany, and many other countries.

Dominating Book Sales

bought the book on Amazon, some of the money made from the sale would go directly to the website owner. Website owners were given anywhere from 3 to 8 percent of the money earned by a book sale made this way. Money made through ads placed on an owner's website is known as commission.

Some of the best members of the Associate's Program were other large website owners, such as Yahoo and America Online. Both of these companies joined the program in 1997. Yahoo and America Online were very popular at the time, which gave Amazon even more exposure on the Internet. Other websites Amazon made partnerships with were GeoCities, AltaVista, and Netscape.

The Associates Program continued to grow, and by the end of 1998, it had reached over 50,000 members. Amazon was able to pay Associates more money, too, with some members earning up to 15 percent of the money Amazon made from book sales linked through a member's website. Today, Amazon's Associates Program is still going strong.

GROWING BIGGER YET

Plenty of investors bought shares from Amazon, allowing Jeff to expand the warehouse even more and then open another one in Delaware. Opening a warehouse on the East Coast meant that customers on the Eastern side of the United States would receive packages even faster than before.

With bigger warehouses, the way orders were filled and shipped changed. Amazon had once needed to wait for books to be shipped to the warehouse after an order was placed, but now Amazon had the space to keep the books that were ordered most often on the warehouse shelves. Many orders placed on Amazon could be shipped the next day.

But this still wasn't fast enough for Jeff. He wanted Amazon to be even faster than that in order to compete with physical bookstores. One of the goals he set for the company was the ability to ship over 90 percent of orders within the same day that the orders were placed. It would take Amazon a while to reach this goal, but Jeff knew it was within reach.

30 AMAZON

Research Project

Using the Internet, research and find all the different companies Amazon.com has bought over the years. List at least five that have not been mentioned in this chapter. What did these companies specialize in? Explain why Amazon needed to buy other companies to become more successful.

Jeff's business plan was working. By 1998, the website was shipping to 160 different countries, which meant Amazon was competing with international companies as well as American ones. Amazon's international customers influenced Jeff's next move.

Amazon made the decision to buy a few smaller international companies in 1998. Some of these companies sold books, while others sold different services or products. One of the businesses Amazon bought was Bookpages.co.uk, a company that sold books to the United Kingdom and other areas of Europe. Amazon renamed it to Amazon UK in October of 1998. Another company Amazon bought was TeleBook, the largest online bookseller in Germany.

A year earlier, Jeff had announced that Amazon.com would soon have one million unique customers. Expanding to the European book market helped Jeff's company reach even higher. By March 1998, Amazon had more than two million customer accounts. Two new programs were launched in 1998 to expand Amazon's **market** even more. The first, known as Amazon Advantage, was aimed at helping independent authors and publishers sell more books than ever before. No longer did publishers have to sell books to the large bookstores to be noticed. Now, all they needed was an account on Amazon.com. The second new program introduced at the same time was Amazon.com Kids. Amazon Kids introduced over 100,000 titles for children and teenagers to choose from.

Dominating Book Sales

31

Text-Dependent Questions

1. Where was Amazon's business first located? Why did Jeff choose this location?
2. How did customers find the books they were looking for on the original Amazon website?
3. When did Amazon officially launch and how many different titles were available on the original website?
4. List examples that show different ways that Amazon grew quickly.
5. Why did Jeff sell part of Amazon.com to shareholders?

It had only taken Amazon a few years to grow from a small garage-based business to one worth millions of dollars. The one million titles Amazon originally offered had now expanded to about 2.5 million. The company was making almost $150 million worth of sales—but it was not yet pulling in a profit. There was still a lot more growing to do!

Words to Understand

venture: Starting to do business in a new, risky area.
media: Information and entertainment that is stored in some way. Music, videos, and books are all media.
digital: Stored on a computer or having to do with computers.

CHAPTER THREE

Expansion

By 1998, Amazon was dominating the book market on a worldwide level. There wasn't much else Jeff could do to expand the company when it came to books. His next move would have to involve selling another product: music! He also announced plans to start selling movies soon after. One of the websites Amazon bought to prepare for the sale of movies was the Internet Movie Database (IMDb).

One of the reasons Jeff chose music and movies as his next **venture** is because many retail bookstores sold music and movies in addition to books. Some of those storefronts were beginning to develop an online store, and Jeff wanted to stay ahead of the game. He couldn't let Amazon lose its competitive edge.

34 AMAZON

Though Amazon started with books, the company eventually started selling a huge number of different products, from movies and music to kitchen supplies and clothes.

Expansion

The Amazon music store opened in June of that year, and over 125,000 titles were immediately available. At the time, compact discs (CDs) were very popular, and most music was sold in that form. Users could listen to short sound clips before buying a CD and having it delivered. The way users found music on the site was very similar to how users found books. They could search by album, artist, song title, or label. Reviews and suggestions were available, too.

In just three short years, Amazon had reached over three million customers and was well on its way to gaining more. A lot of Amazon's success came from Jeff's decisions as the founder and chief executive officer (CEO). He pushed the company to continue growing, even though it still wasn't making a profit. In other words, it was still spending more money than it was bringing in from sales!

Some business analysts doubted Jeff's plan. They believed that all growth and no profit would mean the company would run out of money eventually. Other financial experts thought Jeff would be able to turn a profit before that happened.

HOLIDAY SALES

Jeff was certain he knew what he was doing, and he never stopped preparing for the future. In 1999, he made the decision to start selling toys and electronics on the website in preparation for that year's holiday season. Jeff hoped that shoppers would turn to Amazon.com instead of busy retail stores to get their holiday shopping done. He stocked the Amazon warehouses with over 180 acres of wrapping paper and almost 2,500 miles of ribbon in order to get ready for the winter months. Items ordered through Amazon could be wrapped before they were sent to the customer.

That year, *Time* magazine named Jeff Bezos the Person of the Year. He was given the award because of how he and his company had influenced online shopping. Buying products online was becoming more common than ever before. With any luck, Jeff and his company would see a

36 AMAZON

Amazon's huge holiday sales helped the online store to succeed even more. Black Friday sales and the beginning of Cyber Monday also pushed the company's profits higher.

Expansion

Make Connections

The Friday after Thanksgiving is traditionally known as Black Friday because it is the day shoppers flock to retail stores to get their holiday shopping done. The age of the Internet has changed how shopping is done, however. In 2005, the website Shop.org invented a new term for the Monday after Thanksgiving—Cyber Monday, because people who do their holiday shopping online usually do it on that day. The term has gained popularity and now plenty of websites offer special Cyber Monday sales.

profit by the turn of the century. Unfortunately, there were some problems on the horizon. Jeff would need to work very hard to keep Amazon going strong.

THE INTERNET BUBBLE BURST

Jeff Bezos wasn't the only person trying to make a large, successful website in the 1990s. Plenty of other innovative people had the same idea at about the same time. The creation of commercial websites soared in the late 1990s as companies tried to expand just as Amazon.com was. One website that was starting to gain popularity at the same time as Amazon was Google, which is now one of the most popular search engines on the Internet.

Plenty of online companies were in the same situation as Amazon: they would not make a profit for years. This was a big problem. One financial magazine, *Barron*, predicted that most start-up Internet businesses would run out of money within a year of 2000.

Unfortunately, it turned out that *Barron* was right. Most Internet businesses could not afford to stay in business, and they were quickly going

38 AMAZON

As many new online businesses failed around 2001, Amazon had to cut back to keep the company strong. Though Amazon had to make layoffs, the company survived the Internet Bubble Burst because of quick decision-making.

Expansion

out of business. The competition to stay alive was fierce, and Amazon was one of the few online businesses to survive what became known as the Internet Bubble Burst. One of the reasons Amazon remained strong was the support of its shareholders. People who owned stock in Amazon truly believed in the success of the company, and they kept supporting it even when it was not making any profit.

Surviving the Internet Bubble Burst didn't come without its costs, though. Jeff was forced to lay off 1,300 people and close one of Amazon's distribution facilities. The company also partnered with other websites to offer new deals.

Amazingly, these steps paid off for Amazon. In 2001, when so many Internet businesses were being forced to go out of business, Amazon shareholders finally saw a profit. The company had gained $5 million dollars. Jeff had taken the company in the right direction!

Jeff began focusing on expansion soon after the end of 2001. This time, he introduced clothing to the mix. The focus on expansion caused the company to lose money once more, but Jeff was hopeful. He needed to make his company bigger while he still could, and that meant spreading finances as thin as possible. Amazon did not record another profit until the end of 2002.

With profits back on the map, Amazon.com began expanding its market even further. The website started selling even more products in 2003, including food, sporting equipment, and health-care items. Amazon also bought an online music seller website named CDNow.

KEEPING UP WITH TECHNOLOGY

Expanding its market wasn't the only way Amazon.com was gaining customers. The website was also improving the features it already had. One of the ways buying books was made easier over the years was by providing customers with a way to see inside the book before purchasing it. A few sample pages of a book could be read before spending money

40 AMAZON

Amazon's Kindle helped to change the way people read their favorite books. While customers used to have to wait for the books they ordered from Amazon to come in the mail, e-books allowed readers to get their books right away on their Kindles.

Expansion 41

Make Connections

People have been recording information on some form of paper for thousands of years. Before the invention of the printing press, all books needed to be handwritten. These books were very expensive because of how long they took to make. Only the wealthiest people could afford handwritten books. Common people rarely had books of their own.

The invention of the printing press in the 1400s was an enormous change in the way books were made. Machines could now produce books at a much faster rate, making them more affordable for even the poorest members of society. Printing has improved a lot since then, and by the twentieth century, electronic printers were used to do the job instead of the old printing presses.

But there were more changes ahead. Methods of making and reading books changed dramatically at the beginning of the twenty-first century. Electronic information could now be transferred quickly over the Internet. People could share information from across the world in just seconds. Soon someone invented a way to share books online. These books, known as e-books, are now one of the most popular ways to read a book. E-books can be read on a computer, tablet, smartphone, or any other compatible device.

on the book, just like a small clip of a song could be heard before buying a CD.

Customers were also rewarded for their loyalty with special Amazon.com memberships. At first, students could purchase an Amazon Prime membership for about $80 a year. The membership had certain benefits, one of which was giving members free express shipping for the duration of the membership. Amazon Prime was so popular that it was eventually made available to everyone, and not just student accounts.

Jeff continued his pursuit of owning the company with the world's "Biggest Selection" by launching a jewelry line and forming an alliance with

42 AMAZON

The Kindle was a big change for Amazon. The company had only ever sold other companies' products. With the Kindle, Amazon was beginning to sell it own products through its massive store.

Expansion   43

Text-Dependent Questions

1. Why did Jeff want to start selling movies and music in 1998?
2. Why did Jeff stock the Amazon.com warehouse with wrapping paper and ribbon during the 1999 Holiday season?
3. What is the Internet Bubble Burst and how did Amazon.com survive it?
4. During which year did Amazon.com start making a profit? How long after the company began was this?
5. How people bought media changed a lot in the mid-2000s. How did Amazon.com adapt to this?

the National Basketball Association (NBA) and the Bombay Company. Amazon also set its sights on taking over companies that were going out of business or being sold. During 2005 and 2006, Amazon bought a clothing store, an e-book company, and a print-on-demand company.

Selling *media* for download was just starting to become popular in the mid-2000s. Amazon.com began selling videos for download in 2006. All a user had to do was pay for the item and download it instantly. The videos downloaded from Amazon were of the highest quality, which meant a video bought online would look just as good as a DVD bought from a store. Users could download movies at all hours of the day, removing the need to go to a video store at all.

Electronic books—e-books—started rising in popularity around the same time. Amazon's initial success came from selling books, so it only made sense that the company would jump right into selling e-books. In 2007, Amazon released an e-book reader known as the Kindle. In the modern world, most people believe that faster is always better, and now people could order an e-book online from Amazon and it would be sent straight to their Kindle instantly. The Kindle can store hundreds of books

44 AMAZON

The Kindle was a huge success for Amazon, becoming one of the most popular e-readers available.

Expansion 45

Research Project

Some people think that e-books will one day totally replace paper books. Other people disagree. Use the Internet to find articles that support both viewpoints. Summarize the arguments for each perspective, and then express your own opinions on this topic.

at a time. Downloading books to a Kindle is very simple, and transporting books is easy because of how light the Kindle was.

Next, Amazon introduced a way to download music, known as Amazon MP3, at the end of 2007. This offered a great way for people to download music to their computer, MP3 player, or smartphone.

The *digital* age was officially upon the world. All forms of media could be downloaded, although Amazon still sold physical movies, CDs, and books for those who wanted them.

By this point, Amazon had expanded to many other areas of sales including clothing, shoes, jewelry, sporting goods, food, and personal products. There seemed to be no limit to what Jeff could sell. For him, the sky was the limit, and Amazon was going to find a way to get there.

Words to Understand

applications: Programs that run on a computer or a smartphone. Today, people usually call them "apps."
gigabytes: A way of measuring storage space on a computer. A gigabyte is enough space for about two hundred songs or four hundred pictures.
transforming: Changing into something else.
optimistic: Expecting good things to happen.
prototypes: The first versions of something that you make.

CHAPTER FOUR

Moving Forward

Amazon was very successful and profitable by the late 2000s. The Kindle eReader was doing well, and e-book sales were skyrocketing. Amazon was finally making a steady profit. The only time it lost money was for a brief time in 2012.

BUYING OUT THE COMPETITION

Jeff decided to expand the company even more. His next move was to buy the companies competing with Amazon.

One of the first large companies he bought was Audible, which he bought for $300 million. Audible was a company that sold audiobooks, books that a person could listen to instead of read. Audiobooks can be stored on an MP3 player or CD and listened to in the car, while going for

48 AMAZON

After helping to change reading with the Kindle, Amazon bought audiobook company Audible and started selling audiobooks through its online store.

Moving Forward

> ### Make Connections
>
> Plenty of websites now send e-mails to customers notifying them of upcoming deals or events. These messages help a company bring customers back to the website to make more purchases. Starting in 2008, Amazon even began sending SMS messages to people about the daily deals offered on the website. SMS stands for "short message service." Most people refer to SMS messages as text messages. These text message notifications increased Amazon's traffic and brought in new business.

a run, or while lying in bed. People who are very busy sometimes prefer listening to audiobooks because they are a convenient way to read without actually reading!

Next, in order to keep Amazon Kindle sales going strong, Amazon bought out a company named Stanza in 2009. That company had made an eBook reader similar to the Kindle. Amazon also bought out Lexycle, a company that made software for Stanza. Acquiring Stanza and Lexycle is a good example of Amazon's recent trend of buying out the competition. Jeff decided it was simply easier to buy a competing company than to continue to compete with it.

At about the same time, Amazon began developing **applications** to be used on smartphones. Customers using the application would be able to download e-books from Amazon without actually owning a Kindle device. These applications, or apps, were developed for the iPhone and Android phones. One Kindle application was made for the iPod as well.

Amazon continued expanding its own horizons, now selling a variety of items that had never been seen on the site before. Customers

50 AMAZON

Amazon may have started in a garage, but the company's headquarters today are huge.

Moving Forward

SMART PHONE LAPTOP TABLET OFFICE COMPUTER OTHER DEVICE

CLOUD COMPUTING

With e-books, audiobooks, and digital music and movies, Amazon is moving more and more toward cloud computing, keeping files online until customers want to download their media on their computers, phones, tablets, or other devices.

could now search for cars, motorcycles, and other motor vehicles using Amazon's website. Vehicle parts are also available through the website's online store. As of 2013, there is almost nothing a customer cannot find through Amazon.com.

CONVENIENCE

One of the newest and most exciting features of Amazon.com is Amazon Cloud. Amazon members can use Amazon Cloud to store important information online, including music, movies, and books. Cloud is very

52 AMAZON

Amazon released a tablet computer version of the company's e-reader, called the Kindle Fire. Users can check e-mail, watch movies, listen to music, read books, and search the Internet using the Fire.

Moving Forward

useful for people who need to access files on the go. Users only need to log into their Cloud account to access all the useful information included there.

Being able to access all their media on one website made Amazon even more convenient for customers than it was before. It encouraged Amazon users to buy all their media purchases in one place. Best of all, Cloud was completely free to use for up to five **gigabytes**. Anyone could have an account as long as the software was installed on his or her computer or mobile device.

The original Amazon Kindle was a very successful device for reading e-books, but the future versions were used for much more. Other tablets, such as the Apple iPad, were coming out with features that the original Kindle did not have. Once again, Jeff knew he had to keep up with the competition, so Amazon released the Kindle Fire, a device that can be used to watch videos, browse the Internet, and even record videos using a built-in webcam. Of course, this Kindle is still capable of reading e-books.

All new Kindles come with plenty of storage, and can even access Amazon Cloud, too. Connecting users to all of the products available on Amazon keeps them coming back for more. Amazon will likely continue to follow the changes of technology in an attempt to stay strong. Today, that means catering to smartphone and tablet users. Tomorrow, it might mean something entirely different. It is hard to know how Amazon will keep up with the changing world, but Jeff Bezos will do whatever it takes!

JEFF'S NEW PROJECTS

Jeff has remained the CEO of his company since Amazon began, but that doesn't mean he isn't branching out to other areas of business. One of the ways he has spread his wealth is by starting up a company known as Blue Origin. The company, which first began in 2000, was mostly kept a secret until 2006, when Jeff bought a large amount of land in Texas to host the new venture.

54 AMAZON

Few people could have imagined that one man selling books out of his garage would become one of the world's most successful companies, but Jeff has had an amazing journey with Amazon.

Moving Forward

55

Jeff has had incredible success with Amazon, but now he's looking to find success in spaceflight with his company Blue Origin.

Blue Origin is a project aimed at making spaceflight affordable for the average human being. One of the other goals of the company is to preserve the Earth by finding a realistic way for humans to leave it. The startup company is only in the beginning stages of building spacecraft, but it is already getting off the ground. Blue Origin launched an unmanned rocket ship in 2011, but it was lost during testing.

56 AMAZON

Amazon shows no signs of slowing down in the near future. Today, the company is working on new versions of its Kindle, creating television shows for its online video services, Amazon Instant Video, and thinking of new ways to get products to customers in less time.

Moving Forward   57

Research Project

Using the Internet, find out more about *Star Trek* and its creator Gene Roddenberry. Describe Roddenberry's vision of the future, and explain how Jeff Bezos appears to have absorbed and made real this viewpoint.

Amazon and Blue Origin have kept Jeff busy, but those aren't the only two companies he is managing. He also bought the *Washington Post* in 2013. This newspaper is one of the most popular newspapers in the United States. Jeff had never owned a newspaper before, but as always, he has big ideas and he's excited about trying new things. He told the newspaper's employees:

> The Internet is ***transforming*** almost every element of the news business: shortening news cycles, eroding long-reliable revenue sources, and enabling new kinds of competition, some of which bear little or no news-gathering costs. There is no map, and charting a path ahead will not be easy. We will need to invent, which means we will need to experiment. Our touchstone will be readers, understanding what they care about—government, local leaders, restaurant openings, scout troops, businesses, charities, governors, sports—and working backwards from there. I'm excited and ***optimistic*** about the opportunity for invention.

Another project Jeff has funded is the Clock of the Long Now. This clock, first designed in the 1980s, is meant to continue ticking for thousands of years. Jeff donated $42 million to fund the clock and help the project move forward. Some ***prototypes*** have been made, but the project has not been officially finished.

58   AMAZON

Text-Dependent Questions

1. What is Audible and why did Jeff pay $300 million for it?
2. Why did Amazon develop applications for smartphones? How did it help the company gain more business?
3. What is Amazon Cloud and how is it used?
4. How are the newest Kindles different from the original one? Why were these changes made?
5. What are some big projects Jeff has participated in outside of Amazon? How will these projects help the world become a better place?
6. Based on what you have read in this book, what adjectives would you use to describe Jeff Bezos?

Jeff is often in the news. In early December 2013, he made headlines once again when he revealed a new, experimental Amazon project that he called "Amazon Prime Air." Prime Air will use drones—remote-controlled machines that can perform a range of human tasks—to provide delivery services to customers. According to Jeff, these drones will carry packages weighing up to 5 pounds within a 10-mile distance of the company's distribution centers. He said that Prime Air could become a reality within as little as four or five years!

Jeff's love of science has always shaped his life. As a child he loved the science-fiction TV show *Star Trek*, and perhaps that show is part of why Jeff has always been convinced that truly anything is possible. He is endlessly optimistic, always confident that the future can be built today—and he's not afraid to try new things to make it happen.

Jeff has already proven that science can be used to solve problems and create amazing new products. Who knows what else he will accomplish during his lifetime!

FIND OUT MORE

In Books

Belew, Shannon, and Joel Elad. *Starting an Online Business All-in-One for Dummies*. Hoboken, N.J.: Wiley, 2012.

Byers, Ann. *Jeff Bezos: The Founder of Amazon.com*. New York: Rosen, 2007.

Garty, Judy. *Jeff Bezos: Business Genius of Amazon.com*. Berkeley Heights, N.J.: Enslow, 2003.

Gilbert, Sara. *The Story of Amazon.com*. Mankato, Minn.: Creative Paperbacks, 2013.

Robinson, Tom. *Jeff Bezos: Amazon.com Architect*. Edina, Minn.: ABDO, 2010.

On the Internet

Amazon.com
www.amazon.com

Business Week: "Amazon, the Company That Ate the World"
www.businessweek.com/magazine/the-omnivore-09282011.html

Funding Universe: "Amazon.com, Inc. History"
www.fundinguniverse.com/company-histories/amazon-com-inc-history

Time Magazine: "A Brief History of Online Shopping"
content.time.com/time/business/article/0,8599,2004089,00.html

Time Magazine: "Jeffrey Preston Bezos: 1999 Person of the Year."
content.time.com/time/magazine/article/0,9171,992927,00.html

SERIES GLOSSARY OF KEY TERMS

application: A program that runs on a computer or smartphone. People often call these "apps."

bug: A problem with how a program runs.

byte: A unit of information stored on a computer. One byte is equal to eight digits of binary code—that's eight 1s or 0s.

cloud: Data and apps that are stored on the Internet instead of on your own computer or smartphone are said to be "in the cloud."

data: Information stored on a computer.

debug: Find the problems with an app or program and fix them.

device: Your computer, smartphone, or other piece of technology. Devices can often access the Internet and run apps.

digital: Having to do with computers or stored on a computer.

hardware: The physical part of a computer. The hardware is made up of the parts you can see and touch.

memory: Somewhere that a computer stores information that it is using.

media: Short for multimedia, it's the entertainment or information that can be stored on a computer. Examples of media include music, videos, and e-books.

network: More than one computer or device connected together so information can be shared between them.

pixel: A dot of light or color on a digital display. A computer monitor or phone screen has lots of pixels that work together to create an image.

program: A collection of computer code that does a job.

software: Programs that run on a computer.

technology: Something that people invent to make a job easier or do something new.

INDEX

Abracadabra 17
AltaVista 29
Amazon 7–10, 12–19, 21–31, 33–37, 39–45, 47–58
Amazon Advantage 30
Amazon.com 7, 9, 16, 19, 23, 25, 27, 30–31, 35, 37, 39, 41, 43, 51
Amazon.com Kids 30
Amazon MP3 45
Amazon Prime 41, 58
Amazon Prime Air 58
Amazon River 19
America Online 29
American Booksellers Association 23
Android (phone) 49
Apple Computers 23
applications (apps) 46, 49, 58
Associates Program 27, 29
Audible 47–48, 58
audiobooks 47–49, 51

Barron (magazine) 37
Barton-Davis, Paul 23
Black Friday 36–37
Blue Origin 53, 55, 57
Bombay Company 43
Bookpages.co.uk 30

Cadabra, Inc. 17
CDNow 39
Clock of the Long Now 57
Cloud (Amazon) 51, 53, 58
college 11
compact disc 13, 35
computer 11, 13, 23, 32, 41, 45–46, 52–53
Cyber Monday 36–37

discount 25
drones 58

e-book 19, 43, 47
employee 15, 21, 23, 25, 57

father 11

garage 11, 22–25, 31, 50, 54
GeoCities 29
Google 37

high school 11

Internet 7–8, 10, 13, 19, 29–30, 33, 37, 39, 41, 43, 45, 52–53, 57
Internet Bubble Burst 37, 39, 43
inventory 20, 25

iPad (Apple) 53
iPhone (Apple) 49

Kaphan, Shel 23
Kindle 19, 40, 42–45, 47–49, 52–53, 56
Lexycle 49

mother 11
movie 33
music 32–35, 39, 43, 45, 51–52

National Basketball Association (NBA) 43
Netscape 25, 29

Person of the Year (*Time*) 35
personal computer 11
printing press 41
prototype 46, 57

reviews 27, 35

salary 21
shareholders 31, 39
Silicon Valley 13, 15
smartphones 41, 45–46, 49, 53, 58
SMS messages 49
Stanza 49
Star Trek 57–58
storefronts 22, 33

tablet 41, 52–53
technology 15, 39, 53
TeleBook 30
Time 35

video 13, 32, 43, 53, 56

warehouse 13–15, 29, 35, 43
Washington Post 57
webcam 53

Yahoo 25, 29

ABOUT THE AUTHOR

Aurelia Jackson is a writer living and working in New York City. She has a passion for writing and a love of education, both of which she brings to all the work she does.

PICTURE CREDITS

Dreamstime.com:
6: Frank Gärtner
10: Anton Starikov
12: Wing Ho Tsang
14: Vladek
15: Michael Ledray
16: Francesco Alessi
18: Cosmin - Constantin Sava
20: Bjørn Hovdal
22: Danieloizo
24: Daniel Krylov
26: Ron Sumners
28: Frank Gärtner
32: Steven Brandt
34: Lucian Milasan
36: Yukchong Kwan
38: Robertlamphoto
40: Lucian Milasan
42: Alexiszp
44: Raluca Tudor
46: Lucian Milasan
48: Dododidi
50: Shiningcolors
51: Martinmark
52: Ajv123ajv
56: Ifeelstock

8: James Duncan Davidson | Flickr.com
54: Steve Jurvetson | Flickr.com
55: Bill Ingalls | NASA.gov